Legacy

Dwane Koppler

© 2021 by Dwane Koppler

Creative and technical support provided by Barbara Quin

No part of this book may be used or reproduced in any manner whatsoever without written permission from the author/publisher except in the case of brief quotations within critical articles or reviews.

Photographs and art sources: Creative Commons Pixabay License Free for commercial use, No attribution required: Front Cover planet and dunes, JannikR64 (Pixabay); Front Cover human silhouettes, Annalist Art and Clker-Free Vector Images (Pixabay); Back Cover planet, Planet Eclipse, ParallelVision (Pixabay).

ISBN: 9798702122427
Imprint: Independently published

e-book version available from Amazon Kindle Books

All rights reserved.

Published in the United States of America

DEDICATION

I was present when Reverend Susan Baggett-Spears delivered her Sunday lesson on world peace that is referenced in "The Great Peace Outbreak of 2028." Her talk was so on-point, clearly expressed and enthusiastically delivered that my mind buzzed with it. I immediately bought a recording of the service so I could listen to it again.

As I thought about her talk over the next few days, I thought how wonderful it would be if everyone in the world could hear it, or at least an exceptionally large number of people. The Hundredth Monkey Principle works! Those thoughts led me to write "The Great Peace Outbreak of 2028." Later, as I re-read my writing and pondered what would change in the world if that happened, I was moved to write "Legacy," which I saw as a natural sequence to a world-wide peace outbreak. I wrote "Mars" as a separate story, but considering the common threads in each of those stories, it seemed proper to combine them into one narration; thus was born this book, which is titled *Legacy* because that is what the sequence describes, a legacy from one generation to another.

For her initial inspiration that brought all of this about, I dedicate this book to Reverend Susan Baggett-Spears, inspiring spiritual leader, wonderful model of how to "walk the talk," and my beloved friend.

Dwane Koppler
Springfield, Missouri,
February 2021

PROLOGUE

*** EXTRA!! ***

DATELINE: Brussels, Belgium, Thursday, September 12, 2030

The International Society of Psychodynamicists (ISP) revealed today that it had conclusively determined a single cause for the incredible "Peace Outbreak" that occurred in the summer of 2028. Although many psychologists and other mental health professionals attributed the Outbreak to a general maturing of mankind – while others attributed it to the "Hundredth Monkey Syndrome" – the ISP scientifically traced its origin to a particular event: A lesson on love delivered on May 8, 2011, by internationally revered Reverend Doctor Susan Baggett-Spears.

At the time, Dr. Baggett-Spears was the spiritual leader of a small church in Springfield, Missouri, USA, little known outside of her immediate location. It has been psychometrically proven, however, that *THAT* talk, delivered to a small, humble congregation, was the impetus for the revolution of human thought that followed just a few years later.

Although we find it hard to believe today, at that time, many nations, religions, and political parties held animosity (check your dictionary for definition) towards those of different persuasions. There were "wars" in which people tried to kill other people for holding different beliefs! The Peace Outbreak was a watershed event that changed forever the future of mankind.

As most people know, in the summer of 2028, peace spread spontaneously across our lovely planet: Crime became a memory; bored policemen turned to other professions. Soldiers – first in the hundreds and then in the thousands – essentially told their commanders, "We will do anything to help people, but we will no longer fight."

The disappearance of crime is well described in this statement by an inner-city inhabitant who had supported himself by stealing cars and mugging tourists:

"I was going to mug a guy one night and, as I looked at him, I suddenly realized that whatever I did to him, I did to myself. I ended up walking home with him and we became good friends."

A former dictator of an African nation reported, "I woke up one morning, looked out my palace window, and realized that I really *wanted* to help my people. So, I emptied my Swiss bank accounts and began to build schools for the children."

With the disappearance of international borders, disbanding of armies, and cessation of security checks at airports, millions of man-hours were diverted to work that enhanced the good of all, resulting in the virtual elimination of hunger and deprivation around the world.

While thousands around the world affirm they were present at that auspicious lesson on May 8, 2011, contemporary church records show attendance could not have been more than a few hundred. One congregant known to have been present said, "As Sue talked, I felt my heart opening up and literally sending waves of love out to the entire world."

Apparently, this factor was repeated many times and eventually was a direct cause of the Peace Outbreak.

The ISP has determined that, after Dr. Baggett-Spears's lesson, many of her congregants bought digital copies of that watershed presentation to share with their friends. The idea of loving each other unconditionally began spreading across the globe with exponentially increasing speed.

Increasing requests to hear more of lessons by Dr. Baggett-Spears resulted in the creation of her well-known Internet-based church that today spans the globe.

Although she eschewed formal ordination in the early years of her ministry, her work toward increasing love and understanding in the world led to the granting of a Doctor of Divinity degree by Harvard Divinity School in 2026.

As a result of the ISP's determination, Dr. Baggett-Spears will be awarded the Nobel Peace Prize in Stockholm, Sweden, next spring.

When a reporter told Dr. Baggett-Spears of her impending award, she responded with a gentle smile and said, "God does the work; I'm just a window to His love."

PART I

LEGACY

Peking, Republic of China, 2046

Characters:

- Serena Lambeth, Unity Minister
- Don Lambeth, Licensed Unity Teacher, Serena's husband and coordinator of activities
- Marcia and Marla, "The M&Ms," musicians, singers, and best friends of Don and Serena

Serena exited the transport and stopped on the platform, taking in a deep breath. Don stepped to her side and said, "All okay?"

"Yes," replied Serena, "It's just that I enjoy Peking so much when we come here. The beautiful buildings, the clear air, everything about it."

They stepped aside as Marcia and Marla came up beside them to let other passengers pass by. They stood admiring the beautiful buildings. The synth-marble gleamed in the sunlight, made even more beautiful by the delicate gold and blue trim on the buildings.

Serena continued, "I was reviewing local history while on the flight from St. Louis. I find it hard to believe that only one-hundred years ago, people actually became ill and even died just from breathing the air here! We are so fortunate it is clean now."

"Yes," Don said. "I learned in engineering school about the history of power generation and found it puzzling that it took so long for science to figure out how to capture power from the tides. Of course, ultracapacitors had to be perfected to make that happen."

Marcia chuckled as she nudged Marla and whispered *sotto voce*, "Sure, he knows scientific stuff, but can he sing more than one octave?"

They all laughed. Don said, "That's our shuttle over there, the one flashing the dove insignia on its side. Let's get to the church so we can have everything in place for tonight."

The port opened as they approached; as they settled into the seats, their luggage was being loaded into the cargo pod. The shuttle's computer spoke, "Destination: Unity of Peking. Travel time: Six minutes."

The shuttle lifted smoothly into the sky.

"How do you feel, my love?" Don asked.

"Energized!" replied Serena, "Ready for the weekend! The usual schedule?"

Don nodded as he checked his wristputer. "I'll emcee tonight, and M&M will sing and play five numbers to warm up the audience. Although, from the ovation you got last year, I think they'll already be eager to hear you. You speak tonight, and I'll do the classes tomorrow, with M&M performing after each break for a change of pace. Then, the reception tomorrow night and your lessons Sunday morning. There will be two lessons, with a farewell luncheon afterward. Then, oh, boy! Four days off before going to Sydney on Friday, with the same schedule there. What do you want to do with the off-time?"

Serena grinned at him and said, "I decided that before we left home. Let's go to the Maldives and get some time on the beach. And snorkeling. The water is so gorgeous there! Let's see if we can get our honeymoon hut again. That was such a magical place!"

Don grinned at her; their eyes locked as they communicated in their own language.

"Okay, kids!" chortled Marla, "Keep your minds on spirituality until Monday!"

They all smiled affectionately at each other and looked out through the transparent walls to enjoy the passing scene.

As Don gazed out, he mused aloud. "We live in such miraculous times! What a convenience to have hypersonic flight! Forty-five minutes from St. Louis is a lot better than our ancestors had it. A hundred years ago, it took *hours* to get here from St. Louis. A hundred years before that, it took weeks in a surface ship. A hundred years before *that*, it took *months*! Can you believe it?"

"So, what's next?" asked the impish Marcia. "One hundred years from now, will it be instantaneous?"

"Probably not, but who knows where more knowledge will take us?"

"The convenience is nice, of course, but I really enjoy the beauty of flight. The stars are so brilliant as we go sub-orbital! I always feel a bit sad when we re-enter the atmosphere and the stars fade out," Serena said.

Marcia and Marla both nodded and spoke in unison, as they often did, "Us, too!"

Marla added, "Our next vacation will be in the Orbital Hilton, and we will just look at stars for two whole weeks! Want to come with us?"

Don and Serena thought a moment, then Serena answered, "We'd love to! Let us know the schedule so we can work it in."

The shuttle voice announced, "Arriving: Unity of Peking."

The shuttle gently touched down and the port opened. As the foursome stepped out, they were greeted by the welcoming group, including the local minister and Board of Trustees.

Serena stepped forward, bowed, and spoke in Mandarin, "I am honored to be in your presence again, Minister Wu Tang! May you receive many blessings!"

Wu Tang replied, "Your visit honors us, Minister Serena Lambeth! May you and your troupe be blessed!" He added in Standard English, "Let us dispense with the formal talk, Serena. It's great to see you again! Welcome to Unity of Peking! With Standard English as the global language, it is beginning to be annoying even to the Chinese to remember how to speak Mandarin."

Serena nodded in agreement, then she and the other three greeted each of the Board members in turn. They all stepped into the elevator to descend into the church.

Once on the main floor, Don went to review details with the head technician; dozens of workers scurried about with their wristputers aglow as they tested and programmed equipment. Marcia and Marla went of check out their instruments and lay out their performance clothing.

Serena glanced around approvingly. "The church is lovely, Wu Tang! How many do you expect for tonight?"

Wu Tang checked his wristputer. "All fifty-thousand seats are spoken for. Of course, there are always last-minute cancellations for various reasons, but we have a stand-by list, so expect every seat to be filled. The holographic simulcasts are great, but people still seem to find it special to actually be physically present at something like this."

Don had returned silently and spoke up from behind them. "It's the special radiance she emits, Wu Tang. I have listened to her for years and still feel it when she speaks. It's not something holograms can emulate."

Wu Tang nodded. "I know. I have felt it, too." He looked at them both and said, "We have things in hand here. You're going to be really busy the next three days. Why not go up to the guest suite and relax until starting time? Your luggage is already there, as well as food and refreshments. I'll see you at five o'clock."

They both nodded in agreement and strolled to the elevator hand-in-hand. Wu Tang looked after them with a happy heart, thinking to himself, "They are so blessed!"

Promptly at 5:00 p.m., Don stepped out on the stage to a warm reception from the packed church. He outlined the schedule for the weekend. He knew they all had it on their wristputers, but they still liked to hear it from the Master of Ceremonies. Then, he introduced Marcia and Marla to an even warmer reception and sat down to watch their performance. They entered the stage, hands joined, with identical costumes and hairdos. Don always enjoyed their performances and thought that the special energy they put out was due in part to the deep love they had for each other, as well as their musical talents. Marcia played a few introductory notes, then Marla began; a few seconds later, their voices joined in song, blending with a unique resonance that sometimes gave him goosebumps.

The audience loved them, too, and the applause grew in volume with each song. When they finished, they did two encores the audience begged for, finally blowing kisses to their fans and leaving the stage, hand-in-hand, as they had entered.

Don stepped to center stage again and addressed the audience, "Well, we do have a speaker tonight if you're not too bored." The crowd laughed and stirred. Most of them knew what was coming. One man jumped to his feet near the front row and shouted, "Se-ren-a! Se-ren-a! Se-ren-a!" Within seconds, everyone was on their feet and the shouts reverberated off the walls.

"Se-ren-a! Se-ren-a! SER-EN-A!!!"

Then Don saw the audience look upward; as he sat down, he looked up to see Serena descending out of manufactured clouds in a make-believe sky, appearing to float down through the air. Don knew she was suspended by virtually invisible carbon fibers that would disconnect when her feet touched the stage floor. Her elegant, elasti-silk gown emphasized her shapely body. The microscopic liquid crystals in the fabric changed color and pattern depending on how she moved. He never tired of seeing her in that fabric. Serena landed lightly, walked to the front of the stage, and gave the audience her most brilliant smile. The crowd roared its approval.

"Who are we?" she asked in what Don called her "power voice."

The crowd roared back, "LOVE!"

"What do we do?" she asked.

"LOVE!" reverberated once again throughout the vast room.

"What is our joy?" came the third question.

"LOVE!" was again the response, even louder than before.

Serena smiled a happy smile and waved the audience to their seats. "Well, you know the right answer! Now, turn to person behind you and tell them you love them!"

Don chuckled as the entire audience turned around and then burst into laughter as they realized they were all looking at someone else's back. It was an old trick but never failed to bring humor to the experience. With the audience thoroughly warmed up and engaged, Serena began her talk in earnest. Don settled back contentedly to watch and listen.

He had witnessed Serena begin speaking before they were married and had been her biggest fan as she became a licensed teacher, then a minister, then a senior minister as her fame grew and satellite churches sprang up in other cities, then in other countries.

Her Sunday lessons and other talks were transmitted to the outlying churches via holographic simulcasts that had been improved to the point that the projected image looked like a real person. Once a year, they took a world tour to visit in person some of the largest churches, a trip that was always special and motivating for them both.

As Serena continued her talk, Don felt the energy as she used her voice, hands, body posture, movements, and the radiance of her own energy to communicate her message in a way that never failed to inspire him. Her talent seemed effortless, but Don knew she spent many hours in preparation for major events like this. There was a screen only she could see that had her notes programmed in. She could control the forward and back or select a different note with subtle pressure of her toes on sensors in her shoes, but he knew that she often spoke from some place within her that generated her special gift; the result was always uplifting and meaningful.

Serena's talk came to its conclusion, she gave a closing blessing to the audience and then stood beaming at them as they celebrated her presentation with thunderous applause. Don joined her, along with Maria, Marla, and Wu Tang as they moved through the crowd to greet as many as possible in the hour allotted for that purpose.

"Oh, my! What a group!" Serena exclaimed as the four of them entered their guest suite near midnight. "I even met people from

Unity of Sydney! They wanted to see us here and then again in Sydney next week. What dedication!"

Don agreed. "One of them told me their new sanctuary will be open for our visit. Finishing touches are being done this week."

Marcia and Marla were enthusiastic, too. "My goodness!" said Marla, "I feel so blessed! My wristputer shows that we sold over fifteen thousand albums to the audience tonight! The net from that will pay for our trip to the Orbital Hilton!"

The four chatted excitedly as they shed clothes and donned loose silk gowns. The warm, soft floor felt wonderful to their tired feet. Their evening clothes went into the apparel chute where they would be cleaned and automatically returned to their respective closets in the suite. After refreshments and a half-hour of reviewing the evening, tiredness reared its head; the M&Ms went to their bedroom and Don and Serena retired to theirs.

Sinking gratefully into the body-conforming bed and nestled together contentedly, Don said tenderly, "Well, my love, get some sleep, because tomorrow morning you have an interview with Worldcast. They deem it so newsworthy that the reporter will actually come in person rather than simulcast as they usually do!"

"Okay," Serena agreed sleepily. "Let's get up and run a few kilometers first. It'll help us adjust to the time zone."

Don agreed. "Interview at ten, so would run at seven and breakfast at eight work for you?"

"Sounds good!" Serena said as she snuggled closer. They smiled at each other and kissed tenderly. "I'd like to look at stars as I fall asleep." Serena said.

Don spoke toward the room's Smart controller, "Sky, please." The ceiling turned transparent, the lights dimmed to reveal the Milky Way and a crescent moon overhead. Serena smiled once more. As her eyes closed, she said happily, "Life is GOOD!"

At ten o'clock the next morning, Serena met with the reporter in a conference room. As soon as she was settled in her seat, the reporter got into his questions.

"You come from a long line of spiritual leaders. I have read the history of your family line and it is fascinating. Your grandmother, Reverend Doctor Susan Baggett-Spears, was responsible for getting Standard English adopted as the global language to further build a sense of community, which it has. She also was responsible for the Great Peace Outbreak of 2028, which caused wars to cease and national borders to disappear. Now, you speak all over the world to huge audiences. To what do you credit the spiritual talents of your family line? Specifically, that all of the famous ones are women?"

Serena replied thoughtfully. "The passion seems to be only in the women, as you said, and it seemed to skip a generation. My mother, for example, is highly intelligent, a great speaker and businesswoman, but has no passion for the spiritual teaching that I and my grandmother were blessed with. Do we need to rest a generation in between? Does a new idea need to mature before we can introduce another major change? I have pondered the question for years with no real answer."

"I've talked to psychologists and biometrists while researching your family line. None of them had a plausible explanation, either. Next, I would like to ask you for your thoughts on why Unity has become one of the major spiritual movements in such a short time? Especially considering that the dogmatic religions such as Islam and Christian fundamentalism was dominant for so many centuries."

Serena replied, "The Great Peace Outbreak of 2028 showed the world that individual spirituality was much more appealing than blindly following a religious dogma. Spirituality FREES the individual rather than confining them to a rigid set of beliefs they must follow. Although the global Unity movement has developed several different versions of practice, they all espouse individual freedom of choice and the realization that ALL people are the beloved children of God, not just those who adhere to a certain dogma. I think the life-enriching appeal of this is why the dogmatic religions have shrunk to a tiny percentage of their size a century ago.

"When Standard English became the global language, the last vestige of "us versus them" disappeared because people could go anywhere in the world and converse with whomever they met. Another factor is the disappearance of poverty that formerly existed. The world is now truly the global village that people began envisioning generations ago."

"The first famous one in your family line was Reverend Doctor Sue Baggett-Spears. What do you think she would think of what you are doing now?"

Serena smiled. "I have read her lesson notes, watched her performances on contemporary videos of the time, and read all of her books. I am emulating her to the best of my ability, and I hope she would be pleased."

The reporter said, "Thank you! One more question. Your ancestor was a world changer. What would you like to leave as your legacy?"

Serena answered readily. "I have been considering this since I first became aware of how amazing my grandmother was, especially after I felt my passion for spiritual teaching come alive. I would like to see any religion, indeed ANY human organization that promotes fear, judgmentalism and a rigid doctrine simply disappear into the dustbins of history. My life's purpose is to promote love, mutual respect, acceptance and peace among all human beings. In truth, we are all One!"

"Thank you very much, Reverend Doctor Lambeth!" said the

reporter, touching his ear. "My producer just informed me that your interview had over fifteen million watching from around the world!"

"It was my pleasure!" Serena replied, "I'm grateful for the chance to reach more people!"

As Serena sank into bed next to Don late Sunday night, she sighed deeply.

"Tired?" Don queried gently.

"Yes," Serena said, "Tired, but a *good* tired. I feel happy that everything went so well, and the people were so receptive."

"Went well, indeed!" said Don, "Fifty-thousand attendees in person at each service, with simulcasts going to seven major cities and numerous smaller ones. Millions watched the whole weekend, with countless churches cancelling their own services so they could project you this morning. You are changing lives and changing the world, Serena, and I feel so blessed to be a part of it."

"Thank you," Serena said sweetly, then she pretended gruffness. "Get used to it, Buster, because WHATEVER I do with my life, you WILL be a part of it, so just get used to it!"

Don laughed heartily and reached out to pull Serena close, kissing her soundly.

"Let's see the sky again tonight, please." Serena requested. Don instructed the room controller and stars were once again overhead, with the moon a bit brighter than two nights previous. Serena snuggled closer to Don and reached out to tweak a chest hair. "Woo-hoo! Maldives tomorrow and a full moon Thursday for a midnight beach stroll!" They grinned happily at each other and Serena said, "Life is, indeed, very, VERY GOOD!"

PART II

2057

Mars

Boost in sixty seconds," intoned a neutral voice through the intercom. Darrell Kincaid took a deep breath and reached out to take Shanna Barnes' hand. The acceleration couches were close together, so they sat nearly shoulder to shoulder.

"I love you," he said, "to the depths of my being. No matter how this turns out, know that I'll love you forever!"

Shanna replied, "Yes, I know, and I love you the same, my soul mate!"

Darrell took another breath and tried to relax. The years of training and painful good-byes to family, friends, and Earth itself, had not prepared him totally for this moment.

"Thirty seconds," came the announcement.

"Thank you, Darrell, for the love and joy of our time together. I feel so blessed by it," Shanna said softly.

"Me, too, Shanna," replied Darrell. "If the launch fails, we will be together in Spirit."

Shanna sighed, exclaiming, "Well, it's too late to back out now!"

"Ten seconds," came the voice, then counting down, "Nine… eight… seven… six… …"

Darrell gulped and whispered fiercely, "Love you, Shanna!"

"Love you, Darrel!" Shanna quickly replied.

The next sound they heard was, "Zero… Launch!" from the intercom speaker, and they felt the G-force build until they blacked out.

Darrell dreamt he was swimming with Shanna in the beautiful, clear waters of the Crystal River in Florida, nude, as was their preference. Just as he reached out to bring her closer for a kiss, a voice intruded, "Thrust terminated. Zero G's. Unbuckle at will."

Darrell felt the lightness of his body and memory returned. They had left orbit! Mars Colony Mission #1 was underway!

As Darrell unbuckled his couch harness, Shanna did the same. They floated slightly above the couches as they looked at each other with a grin. The first few minutes of freefall were always a treat, like an exciting carnival ride. Shanna suddenly looked solemn and Darrell intuitively shared the feeling. They would never again experience a carnival ride or anything else of the Earth that had been their home.

Their thoughts were interrupted by the voice over the intercom, "All hands not on critical duty report to the common area."

Darrell joined hands with Shanna, and they made their way through the ship toward the common area.

The common area was the ship's focal point: Dining room, recreation room, conference room, emergency surgery room, etc., serving many needs of the mission. As Darrell and Shanna entered the area, others were also arriving from different parts of the ship. Many were couples, hand-in-hand as Darrell and Shanna were, but there were also singles, both male and female. "Spares," Darrell thought to himself as he briefly contemplated the possibility of death for any of them along the way, and especially once they were on the Martian surface.

Captain Ricardo Almondo floated near the coffee dispenser, his second-in-command nearby.

"Come on in!" he called out. "Find something to anchor to and let's get this meeting underway!"

Darrell noticed that several came in with vomit stains on the front of their space coveralls. He surmised that the stress of launch, more mental than physical, had taken its toll on them.

The wall screen showed that all non-critical members of the mission were present, as documented by their implanted microchips.

Captain Almondo spoke: "No pretentious speeches here, people. You all know our situation. First colonists to Mars, experimental nuclear drive, etc. Questionable long-term success potential. I have just one point to make: Regardless of how this mission turns out, success or total failure, we are in it together! If you do not agree with this, you should have opted out." Numerous voices murmured in agreement.

"All right, from now on, it's all for one, one for all, just like the Three Musketeers, agreed?"

The gathering responded with boisterous shouts of agreement.

"Okay," said the Captain as they quieted down, "You all know the mission profile, so I won't reiterate it. Meeting dismissed!"

After greeting several friends and exchanging encouraging words, Darrell and Shanna returned to their tiny cubicle. Most mission specialists were in wardrooms, but they had scored a tiny nook just large enough for two acceleration couches. They called it their *boudoir*. Both clipped to the couches so they wouldn't float around and faced each other with solemn faces.

"This is really happening!" exclaimed Shanna.

"Yes," replied Darrell. "It is indeed!"

The years of intensive training had been grueling, but nothing could prepare them for the real thing. They still felt a sense of unreality, but their practical side began to kick in. Shanna checked her wristputer and said, "I don't start my duties as navigation officer until a week from now. When do you go on duty?"

Darrell replied, "Five days."

They smiled at each other. "How shall we ever pass the time?" asked Shanna as she grinned big.

"I'll think of something!" replied Darrell as he pulled her close.

Ship routine fell into place and the "days" passed quickly. With no sunrise and sunset, "days" were marked only by the chronometer on the bridge, with the signal sent to everyone's wristputer. Cleaning, minor maintenance, radio contact with Earth, laundry, etc., were shared equally among the mission members. Darrell later thought the dull routine made the time go quicker, perhaps a psychological ploy devised by mission planners.

They had one death en route, a biologist from Italy who became increasingly agitated and eventually found something sharp enough to open his carotid artery. Darrell and Shanna both volunteered to help clean up the cubicle, though it was a daunting task.

As Mars neared, mission members became increasingly somber or excited, depending on their nature.

Every mission member had at least two skills, some had three. Darrell's skills were equipment maintenance and hydroponicist. In addition to navigation officer, Shanna was also a medical technician. She had a third, unofficial skill: a lovely singing voice; sometimes, she entertained a group with her vocal magic. In his maintenance capacity, Darrell would periodically don a space suit and do an EVA to examine the equipment and supply pods on the outside of the ship. Weekly, he was scheduled to check over the Mars habitation module that projected like a huge proboscis from the front of the ship.

While Darrell performed his duties, Shanna would schedule a few hours to continue her perpetual round of checking each mission member for possible disease or infection that might have been caused by a last-minute contamination before they left Earth. They were to be cautious about crowds and public facilities the last few weeks groundside, but Darrell had heard one man bragging about making love to a different woman every night his last two weeks on Earth. Shanna and the other medical people on board would do all they could to ensure that no harmful bacteria or virus was carried by them to the surface of Mars.

Darrell sighed and tapped his screen to turn it off. Shanna felt his movement and turned hers off, too, removing her virtual reality glasses and glancing at him quizzically. "Finished?" she asked.

"Yes," replied Darrell. "It was fascinating! Just think, Ray Bradbury wrote *The Martian Chronicles* over one hundred years ago! They didn't even have Earth satellites then! He had a great imagination, but sure missed the mark on some of the details. He thought they would colonize Mars with chemical rockets. He wrote that someone would walk around Mars planting tree seeds and they would spring up quickly, generating an oxygen atmosphere in no time.”

“Really?” asked Shanna.

“Yes,” answered Darrell. “With over one hundred years of scientific progress, the best we can come up with is genetically modified microbes to break down carbonates in the soil and *hope* that calculations are correct, and the released products will generate enough oxygen in perhaps fifty-to-eighty years that we, or at least our grandkids, will be able to go outside at least briefly without space suits or oxygen masks.”

“The water from the process will help block radiation, so it sounds promising.” Shanna nodded thoughtfully. “I hope we live to see it.”

Darrell touched her hand tenderly. “Me too, my love.”

To change the somber moods they were both experiencing, Darrell asked, “What were you watching?”

Shanna brightened and smiled. “Oh! I just watched an awesome lesson by a minister at our church from long, long ago! It was SO touching!”

“Would that be The Reverend Doctor Baggett-Spears?” asked Darrell.

“Yes,” replied Shanna, “My great-grandmother herself. She was outstanding, even in her nineties. There must have been a special gene that got passed down, because I identify with her SO much!”

“How many did you download?”

“Fifty years of lessons,” replied Shanna, “Enough to watch one a week for fifty years. All of mom’s, and all her grandmother’s that were on video, plus a few other favorite speakers. It won’t be the same as *being* there, of course, no hugs for one thing, but the VR glasses work really well, so it *looks* to the eye like I'm really in the congregation!"

Darrell grinned. "I'll put on my VR glasses and watch the next one with you. That way, you'll get at least *one* hug!"

"Thanks," said Shanna. "It's always good to share the experience. Reading the *Daily Word* together is great, too! I also have fifty years of those. If we live long enough to see them all, we'll just have to start over!"

"Good," quipped Darrell. "It's always good to plan ahead!"

Darrell stroked his beard as he studied the maintenance manual. After weeks in space, several of the crew had decided to grow beards, but they had to comply with length limits for safety reasons. Darrell thought stroking his modest beard helped him concentrate as he looked at oxygenator diagrams to solve a minor glitch.

He glanced up as Shanna entered the cubicle with a mischievous grin on her face. She carefully removed the computer from his lap, saved the program, then straddled him, and kissed him soundly.

"Well, you goat," she chortled. "You have knocked me up! Doc says it will arrive ninety-two days after we land on Mars!"

Darrell stared at her, then grinned big and hugged her tightly.

"You're the first one to be pregnant!" he said wonderingly. "*Our* first child will be the very first native-born Martian in our colony!"

Shanna nodded excitedly. "I thought others would be first, but it turned out almost all of them had long-term birth control implants, so they wouldn't get pregnant until after we actually landed."

Darrell kissed her again and said, "Future Martian Mom, you'll be famous back on Earth, but it won't get you any riches on Mars."

"I know," she replied. "That's not important anyway. What *is* important is that we will be together as a family. How many kids did you say you wanted?" They both laughed, then chuckled, then grew silent as they held each other tightly and contemplated their future.

The great ship sailed backwards silently through space, its fusion engine emitting constant force to slow its velocity to one that would permit entry into a stable orbit of Mars. "Ship" was used to describe it, but it was like no ship most people would visualize. Given the vacuum of space, there was no need for streamlining. What there was a need for was mass balance. Without that, when the engine fired, it moved in a curve. Of course, side jets could have corrected the curve, but designing engineers calculated that balancing mass would be much more efficient and simpler, with only a few side jets for small corrections to the course. It was a motley collection of tubes, squares, globes and other shapes, all fastened together to ensure a precise center of mass for thrust calculations. Hundreds of engineers had worked for years to determine the exact placement of every piece of equipment. Everything from nuclear reactors to cables for securing com antennas had to be carefully considered for mass and distance from the engine thrust line.

The result resembled a grotesque piece of modern art, with objects fastened to the periphery of the drive unit based on careful calculations of mass and distance from thrust line, with no consideration of esthetics. The calculations had proven correct and the ship handled as designed. Rather than using full thrust, as they had leaving Earth orbit, thrust was set to generate a G-force in the ship to match Mars gravity, only 38% of Earth's; thus, mission members could get accustomed again to gravity before they reached Mars.

Darrell and Shanna stood in the Commons with their arms around each other, gazing at the viewscreen.

"Home," said Darrell quietly. "Another three days to orbit, a week to let the Advance Party land Mars habitat and get it operational, then *we* shuttle to the surface, to our new home."

Shanna nodded. "Well, we're together, my love. Whatever may come, we're together."

The red planet loomed large on the screen and they could identify large landmarks they had studied in photographs for years. It was beautiful, but barren.

They hugged each other tightly. Suddenly, Shanna gasped and grabbed her belly.

"Oh! She kicked! I think she's excited about seeing her home!"

Darrell chuckled and patted Shanna's swollen belly gently. "Welcome home, Susan Kincaid-Barnes!"

The Advance Party had done very well. Mars Habitat #1 was up and running only three days after landing. The initial supply module had landed, and Habitat was stocked for occupation. Darrell and Shanna were in the next group to land and excitedly carried their personal belongings to their assigned quarters, which would likely be their home for the rest of their lives.

Initially, Shanna was disappointed with the stark, small space, especially with a child coming on, but took a courageous breath and reminded herself that she had agreed to accept it. She and Darrell chatted as they sought to organize their meager possessions into the all-too-few cabinets. They sighed, looking at the *toilet* they would have to transport to the recycling center every three days. Water and nutrients were too important to waste! Within a few days their urine would be recycled to the water reserve. The solid matter would be used by the hydroponicists to grow food in the farm modules. They sank down on the narrow bed together and sighed again. It had been a *long* day! After months in space, they were now on the alien planet where they had chosen to spend the rest of their lives. Like it or not, they were home.

The crowd in the Community Center was noisy, with excited banter going back and forth. Although larger than the common area on the ship, the Community Center was similar in purpose. It was gathering place, entertainment center, dining hall, etc. Habitat space was limited, so almost every room other than living quarters had two or more purposes.

"Quiet!" the Mission Commander called out. "All of you need to hear this!" The tumult gradually settled. He continued, "Okay, we're on Mars!"

A cheer erupted from the gathering.

"We're here," he continued, "for the rest of our lives. Let's get serious for a moment."

The crowd quieted and grew somber. The Mission Commander continued, "You are all in your assigned spaces and I want to hear NO MORE BITCHING! You agreed to this, you are here, and this *is* your life. Accept it!"

Heads nodded, although some did so grudgingly. The Commander went on, "Duty rosters have been established and will be on your personal 'puters. For the next few months, at least, make scheduled meals or go hungry. After that, we'll try to be more flexible. The next supply module will arrive in six months, but until then, we are making do with what we brought. *Verstehen Sie?*" The German expression from the obviously Latino man brought a few chuckles from the group.

"The re-supply mission is underway already. We can expect a shipment every six months for the first two years, then one every year after that, because we should have our hydroponics farms up and running enough to supply most of our food needs. We are constantly providing input to adjust what, how much, and with what frequency things are added to the re-supply. One thing I personally requested is a supply of Scotch whiskey to celebrate our first year on Mars!" A huge cheer went up in the room.

"One last detail," he said. "The first excursion party has been selected by lot. They are: Richard Jackson, Melanie Carter, Rudi Ebling, Clyde Davis, Darrell Kincaid, Shanna Barnes." There were cheers and groans from the audience. Everyone wanted to be in the first party to venture outside, but only six at a time were allotted. Darrell and Shanna had put their names in early on in hopes it would help their chances.

"Okay!" the Commander said. "Meeting dismissed!"

Darrell and Shanna were last out of the airlock, although they had been first to arrive. They blinked as their visors darkened to block the intense sunlight.

"Wow!" Shanna exclaimed. "The Sahara was nothing like this!"

"Yes," said Darrell. "With the atmosphere so thin, radiation in all frequencies is intense."

They walked a few meters out, silently surveying the landscape. Sand, rocks, and hills stretched to the horizon in all directions, but there was no sign of water or vegetation. After a few minutes, Shanna queried, "You believe you can change this?"

"Yes," Darrell replied confidently. "We have already released the genetically modified organisms that will break down the soil to produce water, oxygen, and other products. We hope they will reproduce exponentially and eventually release enough oxygen and water that we can grow plants, then crops, then have enough atmosphere that our grandkids can be outside without pressure suits. Since the Martian atmosphere is a near vacuum at sixty-some below zero, we have a long way to go. At least fifty years, perhaps eighty, maybe even a hundred. We won't really know how well the organisms are doing until we get measurable results."

Shanna pondered that a moment.

"So, we may or may not live long enough to walk outside without a suit?"

"Yes," Darrell replied somberly. "Perhaps that long."

Shanna screamed and arched her body. Darrell awoke from his nap and jumped up from his chair. The med tech was checking Shanna's pulse and wiping her brow.

"What? WHAT???" he exclaimed.

Shanna took a deep breath and replied, "A big one, Darrell. I think she's ready for life!"

Darrell stuttered helplessly. "Wh-wh-what can I do?" he asked frantically.

"Nothing," Shanna replied with a strained grin, "I have to do this part by myself." She convulsed again as the medic checked the monitors.

Darrell exclaimed, "Love you, Shanna, more than I can say!"

She replied, "I know. Love you, too, but right now I have to birth our daughter."

She gave another yell, arched high and a head appeared between her legs. Darrell thought he would faint. A few minutes later, their daughter was born, cleaned, and placed in Shanna's arms. Shanna and Darrell gazed with rapture at the tiny, sweet face.

"Welcome to your Mars home," said Shanna. Darrell nodded and spoke softly, "We love you, Susan Kincaid-Barnes!"

Darrell and Shanna sat quietly on the bench, holding hands. They looked around the park, relishing the sight of flowers, trees and grass.

"It's lovely." Shanna sighed. "I never thought I would ever see a sight like this again! Thank you, Darrell!"

Darrell chuckled. "It wasn't just me, my love. It was me *plus* the other colony botanists *plus* hundreds of biologists back on Earth who figured out how to do it. The improved seeds from the re-supply missions saved us from the disaster of the batch we brought with us.

"Yes, I know," replied Shanna. "But, still, if you hadn't persisted in changing the genetic makeup of the terra-forming bacteria, *this* wouldn't have been possible in our lifetimes."

"Thank you," conceded Darrell. "It has been a great satisfaction to me that we lived long enough to once again walk on grass and sit outside without pressure suits."

Shanna smiled and rested her head on his shoulder, her silver hair partially obscuring her still beautiful eyes. "I love you, Darrell," she said. "My handsome Martian pioneer!"

"Yep," chuckled Darrell. "That's me! Intrepid pioneer! High blood pressure, failing eyesight, possible prostate cancer. Sturdy pioneer."

"Well, you *are*!" exclaimed Shanna. "Few of the younger people appreciate what we went through to provide the life they have today. The terrible crowding and food rationing when Habitat #1 malfunctioned. The hours working outside in those early pressure suits that chafed so badly.”

“And those horrible dust storms,” added Darrell.

“Oh, yes!” exclaimed Shanna. “They were frightening in summer. Sometimes, I thought they would totally bury us! Then, there were the eyesight problems so many of the First Colony had, including you, poor sweetie. The manufacturers should have known those face shields weren’t blocking all of the frequencies!”

“Let it go, my love,” said Darrell quietly. “We have survived long past our expected lifetimes, and it has been a treasure sharing this life with you!”

Shanna nodded and smiled. “Yes, it has been wonderful, my love. Despite the challenges, I wouldn’t want to have lived this life with anyone but you!”

Darrell grinned and kissed her tenderly. “Me, too, my soul mate!”

They turned their contented gazes to the horizon and contemplated the beautiful sunset.

PART III

2078

Susan Kincaid-Barnes

Sue Kincaid-Barnes adjusted her backpack and took a drink of water as she surveyed the landscape. Baobab trees and bristlecone pines made a beautiful contrast to the red desert. Sparse tufts of thin purple grass added an interesting accent. She checked her wristputer: three miles to First Habitat. It had been a good two days. A solitary hike to Mandela Peak, a campout, then the return hike. It was so nice to get out of First Habitat and away from all the people!

Although Sue had never experienced the spaciousness of Earth, her human nature felt oppressed by the crowding, so she went hiking when possible, preferably alone, since her life was so filled with people when in Habitat. She sometimes hiked locally with her parents but had to go really slow. At seven-foot-six-inches tall, Sue was typical of the First Generation, while most First Settlers were barely over six feet. Although she knew, objectively, that her height was a result of Martian gravity being only a third of what her body was designed to handle, this was all she had known, so it was her normal and she felt sorry for her short parents. Also, they could not stay outside long at all without breathing masks.

She still remembered the first time she had removed her mask outside. It gave her a feeling of euphoria to have her face free of the annoying thing, as well as not having to bother with the oxygen tank. At first, she could only free-breathe for a short while, but as her body adapted and the atmosphere got richer by the year, finally she, and others of the First Generation, could free-breathe indefinitely, so long as they did not over-exert.

The organisms distributed by the First Settlers from orbit had exceeded the planner's wildest dreams. Apparently, they were a perfect match with the Martian soil. Instead of twenty-five years, they had measurable atmospheric oxygen with eighteen months, as well as a trace of water. At five years, clouds would sometimes be seen. At ten years, First Generation kids could go outside briefly, with breathing masks instead of pressure suits.

When Sue crested the last ridge and Habitat came into view, she dropped her backpack and sat on a boulder to take in the view. The huge hydroponics tent still grew most of their food, but as the atmosphere continued to increase in oxygen and water content, more and more crops could be grown outside. By the time *she* had grandchildren, everything would be grown on the burgeoning Martian farms.

Sue contemplated the political turmoil now going on in the Colony. Native-born Martians outnumbered the Colonists and did not have the residual loyalty to Earth, like those who were born there. To them, Mars was home, and they were beginning to chafe at the control Earth still had over Mars.

The calendar was a major source of friction. Earth wanted Mars to follow the Earth calendar, to make record keeping and communications simpler. Days weren't a huge problem, since a day was 24 hours and 37 minutes long. Every forty days was a "Skip Day," to keep days in sync.

Years were another matter. At 687-days for a trip around the sun, keeping Earth years was confusing, considering seasonal climate changes. Some of the more rebellious of the Martian generation had already begun to use a Martian calendar, which in turn irritated the First Settlers quite a bit. They were also talking about declaring Martian independence. They could now grow all of their own food and were even exporting some products and minerals back to Earth. Some plants had mutated in unique ways in the Martian soil and a bored Earth was hungry for uniqueness; thus, the seeds were valuable for trade.

Pockets of rare elements had been discovered that could be mined and shipped back to Earth, which depended heavily on computerization to keep the wheels of society moving. Martian gemstones were a valuable commodity, as their unique colors were highly coveted by the wealthy back on Earth, so they were sold at premium prices. They were easily the most profitable Martian export.

"Well," thought Sue to herself, "we shall see." Privately, she thought the independence movement should be patient and wait until Mars was even more self-sustaining, especially in manufacturing. While simple things were being made there, even surface transport vehicles, more complicated items like electronics and shuttle craft still depended on Earth-side manufacturers.

With a regretful sigh, Sue stood up and donned her backpack to walk the last mile and end her time alone. As she hiked through the powdery sand, she thought of the beauty of the varying shades of purple, orange, green, red and grey. She had seen pictures of sand back on Earth and it seemed all so drab!

Sue was a botanist and teacher in accordance with the Colony practice of each adult having at least two skills. With such a small population, they could not risk having a major tragedy wipe out the availability of a skill necessary to their society's survival, so a computer kept track of what was needed and who had the skill so that a sufficient supply of knowledge could be kept in place.

Although Sue was very adept in both her skills, apparently having inherited her parent's high intelligence, she was most proud of her new recognition as an ordained Unity minister. She had watched videos of her well-known ancestors delivering Sunday lessons and other classes and became so enamored of the messages that she began telling others about the uplifting principles and soon found herself teaching classes while still a teenager. After much wheedling of the Colony Council, she was granted a small ration of time on the communications system so she could correspond with Unity Village on Earth via high-speed data bursts. She sent videos of several her classes to the Village where they were reviewed by a committee of seminary ministers, who were extremely impressed by her zeal and knowledge of Unity principles.

After more instruction via radio, she was certified as a Licensed Unity Teacher and eventually ordained as a minister via radio, a first for the Unity movement. Recognizing the milestone of having the first extra-terrestrial minister, the staff had paid a considerable fee to have FedEx Mars Freight deliver a tangible, paper diploma to Sue, currently displayed with pride on the wall of the Colony's auditorium where she presented lessons, gave classes, and counseled people.

Sue had taken the honor in stride. "How could I *not* know these principles?" she remarked to her parents. "I've had the very best examples to follow!"

The lessons and classes she had watched and re-watched from a young age were by her two namesakes: Reverend Doctor Susan Baggett-Spears, and her own grandmother, Reverend Doctor Serena Lambeth. They were much better than the teachers at Unity Village, she had decided. The teachers tended to be dry and pedantic, while her namesakes radiated energy with their vibrant personalities, lively eyes, and lilting voices.

Approaching the Habitat airlock, she mused, "How funny! Some of those old folks still thought they couldn't go outside without a pressure suit!"

She entered the airlock and gazed around at the familiar surroundings. It was good to be home!

EPILOGUE

2099

Susan Kincaid-Barnes surveyed the room as she wiped tears from her eyes. She knew the huge crowd was partially a result of her parents being the last of the Original Colony, but she knew also that many more were here because they had been well known and respected by Marsopolis citizens as prime architects of the beautiful world that now existed. Few could really visualize the hostile planet upon which the Original Colony had landed and turned into the present-day beauty.

Sue knew because she had not only heard her parents talk about it endlessly, she had also watched all the early videos they had recorded on their 'puters. Her attention was diverted by a couple of kids running around the room giggling.

"Krista! Josh!" she said gently, but firmly. "Quiet down! This is a funeral!"

"Sorry, Grandma," Krista said sheepishly. She took Josh by the hand. "Come on, Bro," she said, "Let's go get some punch!"

Sue smiled and her heart sang. "Those kids!" she thought. "*I love them so much!*"

Continuing to make her way across the room, Sue graciously greeted people as they approached her. The Mayor, Chief Scientist, and other social leaders vied for her attention. She eventually reached the two caskets and stood silently as the crowd withdrew a bit to respect her mourning. She looked at the two aged, shriveled bodies but in her mind's eye, she saw the vibrant, energetic pioneers her parents had been.

They were the last of the Originals, but in Sue's mind, they were the epitome of the Originals. Courageous, highly accomplished, honored by their peers, Darrell Kincaid and Shanna Barnes had been outstanding examples of the true pioneer spirit. Sue thought of the word "pioneer," and wondered what the pioneers on Earth who had settled the Western United States would think of the lives her parents had lived.

"They couldn't imagine it," she decided. As she gazed lovingly at the face of each of her parents in turn, Sue was grateful. "They loved each other so much," she thought to herself. "It's best they went together."

Darrell had died first, of heart failure, in their stone home, the very first home to be built outside the Habitat. Shanna had sat all that first day, holding his hand and weeping. Sue had finally convinced her to go to bed late that night. By the next morning, Shanna was gone, too. "A broken heart," thought Sue. "How wonderful for them to go together!" She sighed deeply, wiped her eyes, and turned again to survey the room. She smiled bravely and extended her hand to the first in the waiting line of mourners.

"Thank you," she said graciously. "My parents would be so grateful you're here!"

The End

ABOUT THE AUTHOR

DWANE KOPPLER has had a variety of jobs and businesses, including dialysis technician, pharmacy technician, commercial pilot, university instructor, motivational speaker, landlord, and housing renovator. He has been writing short stories, poetry, and songs – mostly for his own amusement – for about 40 years. A few of those have been published, but most were just shared with friends. This is his first book, with another under way that will be a collection of poetry, short stories, and songs.

Now retired, Dwane plans to continue writing, and will revive a long-dormant hobby of making metal-art from rescued objects.

www.ingramcontent.com/pod-product-compliance
Lightning Source LLC
Chambersburg PA
CBHW072142150726
48002CB00004B/1591